Samuel French Acting Edition

I0591724

A Bench in the Shade

by Ron Clark

SAMUELFRENCH.COM   SAMUELFRENCH.CO.UK

Copyright © 2018 by Ron Clark
All Rights Reserved

A BENCH IN THE SHADE is fully protected under the copyright laws of the United States of America, the British Commonwealth, including Canada, and all other countries of the Copyright Union. All rights, including professional and amateur stage productions, recitation, lecturing, public reading, motion picture, radio broadcasting, television and the rights of translation into foreign languages are strictly reserved.

ISBN 978-0-573-70734-6

www.SamuelFrench.com
www.SamuelFrench.co.uk

FOR PRODUCTION ENQUIRIES

UNITED STATES AND CANADA
Info@SamuelFrench.com
1-866-598-8449

UNITED KINGDOM AND EUROPE
Plays@SamuelFrench.co.uk
020-7255-4302

Each title is subject to availability from Samuel French, depending upon country of performance. Please be aware that *A BENCH IN THE SHADE* may not be licensed by Samuel French in your territory. Professional and amateur producers should contact the nearest Samuel French office or licensing partner to verify availability.

CAUTION: Professional and amateur producers are hereby warned that *A BENCH IN THE SHADE* is subject to a licensing fee. Publication of this play(s) does not imply availability for performance. Both amateurs and professionals considering a production are strongly advised to apply to Samuel French before starting rehearsals, advertising, or booking a theatre. A licensing fee must be paid whether the title(s) is presented for charity or gain and whether or not admission is charged. Professional/ Stock licensing fees are quoted upon application to Samuel French.

No one shall make any changes in this title(s) for the purpose of production. No part of this book may be reproduced, stored in a retrieval system, or transmitted in any form, by any means, now known or yet to be invented, including mechanical, electronic, photocopying, recording, videotaping, or otherwise, without the prior written permission of the publisher. No one shall upload this title(s), or part of this title(s), to any social media websites.

For all enquiries regarding motion picture, television, and other media rights, please contact Samuel French.

MUSIC USE NOTE

Licensees are solely responsible for obtaining formal written permission from copyright owners to use copyrighted music in the performance of this play and are strongly cautioned to do so. If no such permission is obtained by the licensee, then the licensee must use only original music that the licensee owns and controls. Licensees are solely responsible and liable for all music clearances and shall indemnify the copyright owners of the play(s) and their licensing agent, Samuel French, against any costs, expenses, losses and liabilities arising from the use of music by licensees. Please contact the appropriate music licensing authority in your territory for the rights to any incidental music.

IMPORTANT BILLING AND CREDIT REQUIREMENTS

If you have obtained performance rights to this title, please refer to your licensing agreement for important billing and credit requirements.

CHARACTERS

PAUL
ANNIE
ROBERTO

TIME

The present

AUTHOR'S NOTE

The three characters need not be in their seventies.
They could easily be younger with a few minor changes in the text.

Scene One

(In the dark, we hear the sound of chimes.)

ANNOUNCEMENT. *(Voice-over.)* Attention all residents of Seaside Heights Manor! The groundskeepers have asked that those of you using walkers, please stay off the putting green. The extra holes are making the game too easy.

> *(Curtain rises.)*
>
> *(Morning.)*
>
> *(**PAUL**, a man in his seventies, wearing a robe over his pajamas, is seated on a bench on the grounds of the Valley Seaside Heights Manor Retirement Home. He has socks and slippers on his feet. The newspaper he's reading covers his face. A pathway leads to the home itself. There are a number of bushes and plants, along with a tree that provides plenty of shade for the bench. The shrubbery, etc. changes with the seasons. It's almost spring. Sound of birds chirping overhead followed by a "Plop" on his newspaper. **PAUL** lowers his paper and looks skyward.)*

PAUL. And a good morning to you too.

> *(He removes dirtied part of newspaper and places it on the bench next to him.)*

ANNIE. *(Offstage.)* Paul! You're not going to believe what's going on upstairs.

> *(**ANNIE** enters. She's a good-looking woman in her seventies, chic, with energy to spare. **PAUL** lowers his newspaper.)*

(As she sits:)

ANNIE. Mrs. Gerrin ran over old man Fletcher with her wheelchair and then Fletcher hit her with his cane. They're up there treating her right now.

(A beat.)

Oh yes, and the chef has threatened to quit.

PAUL. So it's not all bad news. And what were those sirens I heard before?

ANNIE. That was Mrs. Conway. She found her room too cold so she set fire to it.

PAUL. That works.

(Resumes reading, then:)

Did you remember to move your clock forward?

ANNIE. I'm not doing that anymore.

PAUL. What's so difficult about moving your clock forward once a year?

ANNIE. Why should I lose an hour?

PAUL. You lose an hour now but you get it back later.

ANNIE. What if I'm not here later? I'm not dying an hour short. A lot can happen in an hour. You can fall in love in an hour...

PAUL. You can brush your teeth in an hour...

ANNIE. I'm not doing it and that's final.

(A beat.)

By the way, those men are back.

*(**PAUL** stares at her.)*

You know, those business types who've been hanging around here for the last few weeks.

PAUL. Maybe they're from the heath department, trying to figure out how come we're still alive.

ANNIE. Something's going on, I tell you. I have a good nose for stuff like that. I can smell trouble.

PAUL. *(Indicates paper.)* I don't have to smell it, I read about it.

(Without looking up, he offers **ANNIE** *part of the newspaper.)*

Here.

ANNIE. You know I don't read the paper anymore. Although I have to admit I miss the sports pages.

PAUL. You do?

ANNIE. Yes, I used to like to see who got arrested.

(She sniffs.)

Is that a new shaving lotion?

PAUL. No, it's Vicks Vaporub.

ANNIE. It's very becoming, if you like the smell of medicine cabinets.

PAUL. You can always sit somewhere else.

ANNIE. You know darn well that this is the only bench that's in the shade.

*(***PAUL*** goes back to his newspaper as* **ANNIE** *takes an apple out of her purse.)*

Want an apple?

PAUL. *(Putting down his paper.)* Do you have two of them?

ANNIE. Why, do you want two of them? I offered you an apple, do you want it or not?

PAUL. *(Tapping his tummy.)* I'd better not. My stomach.

ANNIE. If you didn't spend the entire day reading that garbage, your stomach wouldn't be so messed up.

PAUL. I'm not like you, Annie. I like to know what's going on in the world.

ANNIE. You don't get it, do you? It's the same news every day. All they do is change the names.

(She starts chewing her crisp apple.)

PAUL. Do you have to make all that noise?

ANNIE. It's called chewing, remember?

PAUL. What is that supposed to mean?

ANNIE. It means that some of us can still eat solids.

PAUL. *(Reluctant.)* I eat solids!

ANNIE. Pills don't count.

PAUL. People eat too much anyway. There's an article about that very thing in here today. Did you ever stop to think how many meals we consume in a lifetime?

ANNIE. I don't have time. I'm too busy eating.

> *(She takes another bite of her apple.)*

PAUL. Let's say, for the sake of simplification, that we're both eighty.

ANNIE. *(Resentful.)* I'm nowhere near eighty!

PAUL. What are you talking about? You're seventy-seven.

ANNIE. That's closer to seventy-five!

PAUL. *(Using his finger as if it were a pencil.)* Now, three meals a day times three hundred and sixty-five days a year...that's over a thousand meals a year. That's seventy-seven thousand meals you've had so far.

ANNIE. Don't forget the snacks.

> *(She takes another bite.)*

PAUL. Would you mind chewing more quietly while I read my paper?

> *(He goes back to reading as* **ANNIE** *stretches out and takes a deep breath.)*

ANNIE. There's nothing like Spring, is there?

PAUL. *(From behind his paper.)* It's not Spring till tomorrow. If you read the paper, you'd know that.

ANNIE. Why can't you learn to go with the flow? Not worry what the exact days are. In other words, approach life with more "poetry."

PAUL. You can go on with that poetry crap all you want, but it's still not Spring till tomorrow.

ANNIE. What happened to you today? You're even more sour than usual. Something in the news upset you?

PAUL. *Everything* in the news upsets me.

ANNIE. Then don't read it.

PAUL. How can you go through life not knowing what's going on?

ANNIE. I'm in the twilight of my years. I don't have to know what's going on anymore. I can enjoy the scenery, I can bask in the breeze and eat my apple.

> *(She takes one more bite and flings the apple core into nearby trash receptacle and then calls out like a sports announcer:)*

And she scores!

PAUL. *(Lowers newspaper.)* Can I read now?

ANNIE. Be my guest.

> *(A beat.)*

Besides, if I want to know anything all I have to do is take out my phone.

> *(She takes out her iPhone.)*

It does *eveything*. I can check the weather, the time, breaking news, messages, e-mails, Twitter, Snapchat, Facebook, you name it.

PAUL. No, *you* name it. I'm not interested in any of that.

ANNIE. It's the twenty-first century, Paul!

PAUL. Don't remind me.

> *(Goes back to reading.)*

ANNIE. You should get one of these. It has a timer so you won't forget to take your pills. You can play games on it. You can listen to music. You can use it as a flashlight when you get up at night to go to the bathroom.

PAUL. I don't need a flashlight, I leave the lights on.

ANNIE. No wonder you don't sleep at night.

PAUL. Who told you that?

ANNIE. You did. Every day you complain about not sleeping.

PAUL. *(Suspiciously.)* How many hours do you sleep at night?

ANNIE. Eight hours.

PAUL. That's too much. Eight hours a day times three hundred and sixty-five...

ANNIE. You're just jealous. It drives you crazy that I never told you my secret.

PAUL. What secret?

ANNIE. How I fall asleep.

> (**PAUL** *stares at her.*)

Okay, I'll tell you. First of all, I get into bed...

PAUL. That's some secret.

ANNIE. Then I lie on my back, and with my eyes wide open, I count my dead friends.

PAUL. That's cheerful.

ANNIE. I'm not looking for anything cheerful, I'm looking for sleep.

PAUL. *(Incredulous.)* You count your dead friends!

ANNIE. That's right. By the time I get to you, I'm sound asleep.

PAUL. I fail to see the humor in that.

ANNIE. You fail to see the humor in *everything*. That's probably why you became an accountant.

PAUL. Accountants don't have to be funny, as long as they... *(Sways from side to side.)* ...know how to balance.

> *(Laughs.)*

> *(Goes back to reading his paper.)*

ANNIE. There's proof right there.

> *(A beat.)*

What do you think of the new boarder?

PAUL. *(Lowers paper.)* What new boarder?

ANNIE. That new guy who moved in a few days ago. He's an actor, you know.

> *(A beat.)*

Does the name Roberto Delarosa mean anything to you?

PAUL. Never heard of him.

ANNIE. Of course you have, he made several movies with that famous Italian actress...what's her name.

PAUL. Her, I heard of.

ANNIE. I knew today was going to be a special day. My horoscope never lies.

PAUL. Your horoscope never shuts up.

ANNIE. Anyway, he introduced himself to me this morning. I hope you don't mind. I asked him to come join us on the bench.

PAUL. You what?

>   *(Slams his paper down.)*

Shouldn't you check with me before making decisions like that? It's bad luck, three on a bench.

ANNIE. *(Correcting him.)* It's three on a match.

PAUL. Same thing.

ANNIE. *(Sighs.)* I think he's the best-looking man in the entire place.

PAUL. You think every man is good-looking.

ANNIE. *(Looks at him; pointedly.)* There are exceptions.

>   *(A beat.)*

I wonder how he wound up in this place?

PAUL. Oh, this is just a wild guess, but maybe it has something to do with his age.

ANNIE. What's the matter with you? Movie stars don't age, they just grow more "intriguing."

PAUL. Tell me something, Annie, How come, if he's such an "intriguing movie star," he didn't wind up in some fancy actors home?

ANNIE. Maybe he doesn't like actors.

PAUL. Good, that makes two of us.

ANNIE. What have you got against actors?

PAUL. Nothing. If I want to see them, I turn on my TV.

>   *(Indicates with hand.)*

PAUL. If I don't, I give them the clicker.

> *(Indicates with hand.)*

I don't need Hollywood phonies in my life.

ANNIE. Well I do. I think they're fascinating people. Besides I've never made love to an actor.

PAUL. *(Looks at her for a moment.)* I read somewhere that you don't make love to an actor. You have sex with an actor while he talks to his agent.

ANNIE. He doesn't know it yet but he and I have something in common.

> **(PAUL** *looks at her.)*

I dabbled in the theatre.

PAUL. Beauty pageants are not exactly theatre.

ANNIE. They both take place on stage.

> *(Suddenly noticing something in the distance.)*

Oh my God, is that him?

PAUL. Who?

ANNIE. The actor.

PAUL. *(Squinting to see.)* How can you tell from here?

ANNIE. He radiates.

PAUL. Oh good, a radiator. He'll come in handy next winter.

ANNIE. He's looking this way.

PAUL. With the back of his head?

ANNIE. That's not the back of his head. That's the way he wears his hair.

PAUL. Covering his face?

ANNIE. It happens to be very seductive.

PAUL. Who is he trying to seduce, Yorkshire terriers?

ANNIE. He's coming this way. Quick, help me up.

> **(PAUL** *puts newspaper down and starts helping her up.)*

Not like that. Go around this side.

PAUL. Why?

ANNIE. So he won't see you helping me.

(**PAUL** *goes around and tries helping her.*)

PAUL. What is he going to think I'm doing, the Heimlich maneuver?

ANNIE. Just help.

PAUL. You're heavier than I thought.

ANNIE. I'm not heavy, it's gravity.

(**PAUL** *has managed to help her up. Now her derrière is in his face.*)

PAUL. I think I know where your gravity went.

ANNIE. *(Now up, looks off.)* Where'd he go?

PAUL. *(As he sits.)* Maybe he just wanted to see if I could get you up.

ANNIE. You should have helped me faster.

PAUL. Do you plan to remain standing?

ANNIE. Why would I want to remain standing?

PAUL. Just trying to save myself some work.

ANNIE. *(As she sits back down and looks off.)* Is that him over there?

PAUL. *(Squints, looks off.)* That's the mailman.

(*A beat.*)

There is a resemblance though.

(*He turns the pages of his paper several times. The rattling annoys* **ANNIE.**)

ANNIE. I would appreciate it if you made an effort not to rattle the pages like that.

PAUL. Boy, you have some nerve. You show up here every day, late I might add...

ANNIE. What am I late for? To see what pajamas you're wearing today?

PAUL. What's wrong with pajamas?

ANNIE. Every single day?

PAUL. I take a nap in the morning, a nap in the afternoon and a nap before going to bed. Why should I bother dressing and undressing all day long?

ANNIE. Why can't you wear a sports jacket now and then so I'd have something to look at?

PAUL. Don't look.

ANNIE. I'm not asking you to spend a lot of money. Just a nice simple jacket so you could look a little more "presentable"...like yours truly.

PAUL. Who asked you to get dressed up to come meet me?

ANNIE. First of all, I don't dress for you, I dress for myself. Every morning I pick out a nice skirt, a nice top, some jewelry. I even change shoes every day. Then I look in the mirror and I say: "You still got it, gal." That's why I dress. If it happens to cheer up people around me, all the better.

PAUL. I don't need cheering up. All I need are my naps.

(**PAUL** *goes back to his newspaper.* **ANNIE** *continues to look off.*)

ANNIE. Where could he have gone? Why would he come out here, look this way, start toward us, then suddenly disappear? What makes a person do a thing like that? I don't get it. I just don't get it.

PAUL. (*Slams paper down.*) You hate the fact that I like to sit here quietly and read my newspaper. You can't stand it, can you?

ANNIE. You know what your problem is, Paul? You're not at peace with yourself.

PAUL. Oh, I'm at peace with myself, I'm just not at peace with *you*. Why don't you do me a favor and go sit on another bench.

ANNIE. Believe me, if there was another bench in the shade I'd never sit with you.

PAUL. Oh yeah? Then why did you call and insist I come stay here at Seaside Heights Manor?

ANNIE. What are you talking about?

PAUL. You know damn well what I'm talking about. You tracked me down and you called me and said: "Hi Paul, it's Annie. I'm phoning you from a place called Seaside Heights Manor near Asbury Park, New Jersey, and a room just opened up." I didn't even know who you were.

ANNIE. You knew enough to show up.

PAUL. I mean at first I didn't know who you were. I hadn't heard from you in forty years.

ANNIE. Forty-two.

(As if in a trance:)

Forty-two years! What I packed into those years. What memories! You're looking at a very contented woman.

PAUL. I'm not looking.

(He goes back to his newspaper.)

ANNIE. I've had a good life, Paul, and that includes every emotion imaginable. I've been happy, I've been sad. I've been ecstatic, I've been depressed. I've been healthy, I've been sick. I've had terrible shocks, I've had great surprises. I've had ups and I've had downs. I've had it all.

PAUL. So what are you suggesting with that laundry list? Just because I stayed married to *one* woman, lived in *one* house, worked at *one* job all my life, are you suggesting I didn't *live*?

ANNIE. I'm not suggesting anything. I'm just saying that life is a challenge and you've got to challenge it right back. And that's what I did. I tasted life.

PAUL. I tasted it too and I spit it out. You're like a lot of people who review their lives and leave out all the rotten parts.

ANNIE. I'm not leaving out anything. I'm including the three failed marriages *and* the children I never had. All I'm saying is that I'm not afraid to review my life and analyze it. That's the big difference between the two of us. I see life as one big "tableau."

PAUL. Tableau?

ANNIE. Yes, tableau.

> *(During the above,* **ROBERTO** *has entered.*
> **ROBERTO** *is a contemporary of Paul's but
> looks younger and in better shape. He's
> dressed rather nattily with a kerchief in his
> jacket pocket. He speaks with a slight Italian
> accent.)*

ROBERTO. Do I hear French spoken here?

ANNIE. *(All smiles.)* Oh, Roberto, what a nice surprise! I
want you to meet Paul Lipton before he leaves.

PAUL. I'm leaving?

ANNIE. Yes, you had things to do, remember?

PAUL. I did?

ROBERTO. *(Extending his hand.)* A pleasure to meet you,
segnore. Annie told me all about you.

ANNIE. *(To* **PAUL.***)* And he still wanted to meet you.

PAUL. *(As he rises.)* I suppose I should go take my Pepto-
Bismol.

ROBERTO. Before mealtime?

PAUL. It's the least I can do for my stomach.

ROBERTO. I happen to like the food here so far.

PAUL. Oh really? Well, unless you've come directly from
jail, that statement makes no sense whatsoever.

ROBERTO. *(To* **ANNIE.***)* And you said he had no sense of humor.

ANNIE. Wait.

> *(***PAUL** *is about to leave.)*

ROBERTO. *(Holding his hand up.)* Just a moment, please.
You may be interested in hearing this. I spoke to
management last evening.

PAUL. Oh, are we going out on strike?

ROBERTO. I suggested it might be fun if they'd let us have a
dance one of these nights.

ANNIE. That is the single best news I've heard in years. I
can't wait to dress up for this dance.

PAUL. I don't have anything to wear to a dance.

ANNIE. What's the matter, don't you have any party pajamas?

ROBERTO. I also talked to them about taking a day trip to Atlantic City. Do a little gambling, see a show.

ANNIE. I *love* slot machines. I love the noise they make. They're like little piggy banks.

PAUL. Yeah, piggy banks that fill up and run away with your money. I was an accountant. Accountants don't gamble.

ROBERTO. Are they allowed to go see a show?

ANNIE. Say "yes," Paul. Try it, it might be fun.

PAUL. You guys work it out.

>　　　*(He starts to go.)*

ANNIE. *(Calls out.)* Lentil soup today!

PAUL. *(Calling back.)* Did you have to tell me? Half the fun of living here is trying to guess what we just ate.

ROBERTO. Arrivederci!

>　　　*(**PAUL** exits.)*

He's quite a character.

ANNIE. Well, he's been through some rough times. Do you know how far back we go together? Over forty years.

ROBERTO. *(Surprised.)* That long?

ANNIE. We knew each other in Columbus, where we're both from.

>　　　*(With mock pride:)*

I had just been crowned "Miss Ohio" when we met.

ROBERTO. *(Impressed.)* Miss Ohio! And I see on the bulletin board that you were voted Miss Seaside Heights Manor.

ANNIE. *(Laughs.)* Well, there's not a whole lot of competition here.

>　　　*(A beat.)*

Believe it or not, Paul and I were once engaged to be married.

>　　　*(**ROBERTO** stares at her, mouth open.)*

ANNIE. I don't think he ever forgave me for running off with his best friend, the richest boy in town.

ROBERTO. You married his best friend?

ANNIE. Well, he wasn't his best friend after that.

ROBERTO. And now you're here together?

ANNIE. I know. It's crazy, isn't it? A lot happened in between. I married two more rich men.

ROBERTO. Wow. Three for three.

ANNIE. Rich men have a lot in common. They like their women young and pretty and they don't like them to age.

ROBERTO. Rich men are stupid.

ANNIE. They also have a habit of getting caught in bed with their wife's best friend.

ROBERTO. Are you saying that happened all three times?

ANNIE. *(Nods.)* How does that saying go? "What goes around...keeps going around."

ROBERTO. Boy, I thought *I* had marriage stories.

ANNIE. How many times were you married?

ROBERTO. Four.

ANNIE. You win. But then again, you're an actor. It's expected of you. Were any of them actresses?

ROBERTO. Three of them were. An actor should never marry an actress. There just aren't enough mirrors in a house.

ANNIE. *(Laughs.)* Anybody I'd recognize?

ROBERTO. I don't think so. I always made sure I had top billing.

ANNIE. All Italian?

ROBERTO. No, one Italian, one Spanish and one Moroccan. The fourth one was American and she wasn't even in the business. And she was blind.

ANNIE. Really?

ROBERTO. But she saw through me anyway.

ANNIE. Any children?

ROBERTO. Two; a young man and a young woman. I haven't seen either one in over twenty years

ANNIE. Are they here?

ROBERTO. As far as I know, they're still in Italy.

ANNIE. Aren't you dying to see them?

ROBERTO. Yes, but they're not dying to see me.

ANNIE. That bad, huh?

ROBERTO. Plans that didn't quite work out.

ANNIE. I had my share of *those.*

ROBERTO. What about you, did you have any children?

ANNIE. Not a one. I could sure use a couple of kids right now.

ROBERTO. To take care of you?

ANNIE. No, to take care of them.

ROBERTO. Maybe you and I can take care of each other.

ANNIE. *(Looks at him for a moment.)* You Latin types don't waste time, do you?

ROBERTO. *(Gets up.)* It's such a beautiful day. Shall we dine on the terrace?

> *(Extends his hand.)*

Prego.

ANNIE. *(Takes his hand and gets up.)* Grazie.

> *(They start to walk off.)*

ROBERTO. I spoke to the chef last night. I got him to replace the lentil soup with "minestrone."

ANNIE. Life is full of surprises!

> *(Lights fade, followed by musical chimes.)*

ANNOUNCEMENT. *(Voice-over.)* Attention everyone! Once again, may we remind you that there is no smoking on the premises. The only area where smoking is permitted is the area next to the health club. And that goes for the medical staff as well.

Scene Two

(A week later – afternoon.)

*(***ANNIE*** *is standing next to the bench, holding onto it with one hand while extending her other arm outward, stretching and bending and taking deep breaths.* **PAUL** *enters, now wearing regular pants instead of pajamas.)*

PAUL. Why are you standing?

ANNIE. We sit too much. We're always sitting. If we're not sitting out here, we're sitting inside. We sit in our rooms, we sit to eat. All we do is sit. It's not good for the circulation.

PAUL. I would think it would be the opposite. When you're standing your blood goes right down into your feet but when you sit, at least the blood makes a little detour at your knees.

ANNIE. *(Stares at him for a moment.)* You should do some of these exercises.

PAUL. *(He sits.)* I exercise plenty.

ANNIE. Like what?

PAUL. Well, since I started putting pants on every morning, that's forty-five minutes right there.

> *(***ANNIE*** *sits and gathers a nearby yellow pad, takes out a pen.)*

PAUL. What are you doing?

ANNIE. I've started writing my memoirs.

PAUL. Your what?

ANNIE. You know, what we spent a lifetime accumulating.

PAUL. Did you keep a diary?

ANNIE. I don't need a diary. It's all up here.

> *(Indicates her head.)*

PAUL. You should've kept a diary.

> *(A beat.)*

What made you start writing your "memoirs" anyway?

ANNIE. Why not? I'm feeling good. There's a new man in my life.

 (Confidentially:)

He told me he's from a place called Ferrentino, just outside Rome, or, as he calls it, "Roma."

PAUL. *(Making fun of her pronunciation.)* "Roma."

 (Glances at her pad.)

How many pages have you got so far?

ANNIE. Two.

PAUL. Not exactly a load of "memories."

ANNIE. Don't you worry about that. Now, if you don't mind, I'm reviewing an entire lifetime here. I have a lot of work to do. I'm trying to sort out husband number one from husband number two and then there's husband number three.

PAUL. That's real nice, calling your husbands by numbers.

ANNIE. I'm only calling them by numbers because you didn't know them.

PAUL. *(Challenging her.)* I don't think you remember their names.

ANNIE. I certainly do! There was Adam and Bernie and Charles.

PAUL. I notice you stayed at the front of the alphabet.

ANNIE. For your information, there was almost an Xavier in there too, but he got away.

 (Sighs.)

I especially remember Bernie. Having sex with Bernie was like ordering Peking duck. You had to give him two days' notice.

PAUL. You stole that joke from the comedian last week.

ANNIE. So what? You stole one the week before.

PAUL. Which one?

ANNIE. The one about the bank.

PAUL. Oh yeah. "I asked the teller to check my balance. She pushed me."

> (**ANNIE** *puts away her pad and pen.*)

That's it? No more writing?

ANNIE. You'd be surprised what a few pages a day can add up to. Two pages a day times three hundred and sixty-five...

PAUL. Are you planning to work weekends?

ANNIE. A writer works all the time. Weekends, holidays, vacations...

PAUL. You mean to tell me that Shakespeare never took a day off.

ANNIE. How do I know what Shakespeare did? We're not the same type of writer.

PAUL. No kidding. By the way, I did a little research on your "actor" friend. According to his "dossier" he's moved around quite a lot. He's resided at three different homes in the last eighteen months.

ANNIE. Maybe he's been looking for the perfect place.

PAUL. Does Seaside Heights Manor look like the perfect place? We're nowhere near the sea. As for the heights, we're below street level, and calling this place a manor is like me calling my bathroom a villa.

ANNIE. Well I think it's just fine. People complain too much. We should be satisfied with what we have.

PAUL. Is that right? I have an ulcer, weak lungs, a replacement knee and a bad heart. I'm telling you right now, I'm not satisfied.

> (*A beat.*)

I'll bet that's not his own hair.

ANNIE. So he borrowed it from someone.

PAUL. And those aren't his real teeth.

ANNIE. Whose are they, his mother's?

PAUL. That's not his original nose either.

ANNIE. When did you become such an expert?

PAUL. And his face has been pulled back.

ANNIE. Of course his face has been pulled back, he's a movie star.

PAUL. And I guarantee that's not his real name.

ANNIE. All I know is that he's someone I'm very much interested in. And he's obviously interested in me too.

PAUL. Oh, really? I haven't seen him around that much this week.

ANNIE. It's the courting game.

PAUL. Looks more like the rejection game.

ANNIE. Don't you worry about that. Just stay tuned.

PAUL. You mark my words, that man will bring you nothing but trouble.

> *(During the following,* **ANNIE** *reaches into her bag and pulls out a long, bright-red, narrow piece of knitting that reaches halfway to the ground.)*

ANNIE. You know, just because two people sit next to each other doesn't mean they have to talk.

PAUL. That's a great idea. I'll go first.

ANNIE. You'll go first what?

PAUL. I'll go first not talking.

> *(Resumes reading his paper.)*

ANNIE. You're impossible.

PAUL. You talking to me?

ANNIE. You know what I think would be good for you? You should learn to meditate.

PAUL. I'm medicated enough.

ANNIE. *Meditate*, not medicate.

PAUL. If you knew what's going on in the world you'd be too nervous to meditate. They've got platforms floating around the globe, doctors are transplanting body parts willy-nilly and now they're talking about cloning people.

ANNIE. You mean there could be two of you?

PAUL. That's right. By next year I could be sitting on both sides of you. I'm telling you, it's time to pack it in.

ANNIE. Well, when I'm ready to meet my maker, I'll send you a tweet.

PAUL. What are you, a bird?

(*A beat.*)

By the way, have you made arrangements for the "inevitable"?

ANNIE. It's too early to make those plans. What about you?

PAUL. I'm going to be cremated

ANNIE. And where do you want your ashes to go?

PAUL. I couldn't care less.

ANNIE. Don't you want them to go in a special place?

PAUL. They can flush them down the toilet for all I care.

ANNIE. I feel sorry for you.

(*She goes back to her knitting.*)

PAUL. And whatever you do, *please* no eulogy! I hate eulogies. Everybody was the best father, the best husband, the best provider, the best wit. A week before they were calling him an asshole.

(*Notices her knitting.*)

What the hell is that?

ANNIE. It's called knitting. I took a correspondence course last year.

PAUL. Do you think that maybe, some of the lessons got lost in the mail?

ANNIE. What's wrong with it?

PAUL. What made you decide to knit a scarf?

ANNIE. It's not a scarf, it's a sweater.

PAUL. Who for, a baboon?

ANNIE. Actually, it's for Roberto,

PAUL. Perfect!

ROBERTO. (*Offstage.*) Yoo-hoo!

(**ANNIE** *quickly puts her knitting away as* **ROBERTO** *enters, looking as dapper as ever. He's holding what appears to be a large album.*)

There you are.

(*He joins them at the bench, sits next to* **ANNIE.**)

I didn't see you at breakfast this morning.

PAUL. Sure you did. You sat next to me.

ROBERTO. I was talking to Annie.

ANNIE. I wasn't hungry. I had a restless night.

ROBERTO. (*Nudges her playfully.*) Perhaps dreaming about someone special?

ANNIE. Now, you stop that.

PAUL. (*As he gets up.*) I think I'll go eat another breakfast.

ROBERTO. I thought you didn't like the food here.

PAUL. I don't. But it can't be worse than the gooey stuff out here.

(*He exits.*)

ANNIE. (*Calls out.*) Clam chowder today!

PAUL. (*As he exits.*) Good luck finding the clams.

ANNIE. You know what he told me when he got back from his knee operation? "I miss the hospital food."

(*Referring to album:*)

What have you got there?

ROBERTO. (*As he opens his scrapbook.*) I thought you might enjoy leafing through my career.

ANNIE. (*Delighted.*) What fun!

ROBERTO. I'll spare you the really early years.

(*Turns a few pages.*)

This was my very first screen appearance. That's me at seven, and that's Sophia Loren squeezing me into her bosom.

ANNIE. I see you're smiling.

ROBERTO. Yes, even at seven, you know a soft pillow when you see one.

ANNIE. Was she nice?

ROBERTO. The nicest. I played her son. She treated me like I was a star.

> *(Turns page.)*

This is me with Anna Magnani. She was also a big Italian movie queen. I was thirteen here. I played a young thief.

> *(Turns page.)*

And this is when I came to America.

ANNIE. *(Reading.)* Beach Bongo Party.

ROBERTO. They were grooming me to become the next Frankie Avalon. That's me, playing ping-pong with Annette Funicello. She didn't even speak Italian.

ANNIE. *(Turning back a few pages.)* Was that Rock Hudson?

ROBERTO. Yes, we became good friends.

ANNIE. How good?

ROBERTO. No, no, nothing like that. We had the same agent. As you can well imagine, our agent spent a lot more time on Rock's career than on mine.

ANNIE. I'll bet you went to a lot of wild parties.

ROBERTO. Not that many. When you're making films you have to get up at five a.m.

ANNIE. I thought actors and actresses just lounged around swimming pools all day.

ROBERTO. Only the unemployed ones. The rest of us got up at five, sometimes we'd work till eleven, twelve at night and then up again at five the next morning.

ANNIE. Didn't leave you much time for those sordid Hollywood love affairs.

ROBERTO. That's the beauty of sordid love affairs, they don't take much time.

> *(He laughs, she joins him.)*

ANNIE. You're lucky. You had a colorful career.

ROBERTO. Colorful but short. Skinny-dipping with the wife of a studio boss is not a great career builder.

ANNIE. You really are a naughty boy, aren't you? What about all those movies you made in France and in Spain?

ROBERTO. I got most of those because I spoke the language. And there weren't that many.

ANNIE. You're much too humble.

ROBERTO. Don't tell Paul any of this, okay?

ANNIE. Promise.

ROBERTO. Do you think he approves of me?

ANNIE. Who cares?

ROBERTO. I mean the two of you go back so far together.

ANNIE. All we do is argue.

ROBERTO. Yes but sometimes people who argue like that, do it because there's something else going on inside.

ANNIE. Me and Paul? Are you out of your mind?

ROBERTO. Well I'm glad to hear that. Now I can move forward with my plan.

ANNIE. *(Suspicious.)* What plan?

ROBERTO. I think you and I would make a wonderful couple.

ANNIE. A couple of what?

ROBERTO. A couple of happy senior citizens.

ANNIE. Is this a proposal?

ROBERTO. Well, it's more like a proposition.

ANNIE. I remember those. You want to move in with me.

ROBERTO. Or you move in with me.

ANNIE. Either way we'd be in the same room together.

ROBERTO. That's the general idea.

ANNIE. *(Shakes her head.)* Sorry.

ROBERTO. But I thought we had something special going.

ANNIE. We do. And the reason we do is because we live in separate rooms. I'm getting too old to start bumping into people. I bruise too easily.

ROBERTO. I'd be very careful.

ANNIE. *(Takes his hand.)* Roberto, you're very sweet but after years of being independent it's very hard to turn the clock back. We'd only get on each other's nerves.

ROBERTO. What if I asked you to marry me?

ANNIE. *(A beat.)* Let's see now, your four plus my three and now this one would make eight. Eight is not a lucky number.

ROBERTO. Says who?

ANNIE. Says me.

ROBERTO. But Annie, we're not going to live forever.

ANNIE. Speak for yourself. I intend to go way past a hundred.

ROBERTO. Alone?

ANNIE. Not alone. I have you upstairs, six rooms down the hall.

ROBERTO. *(Correcting her.)* Five.

ANNIE. See that? We're even closer than I thought.

ROBERTO. So I take it, that's an official turn-down.

ANNIE. Don't think of it as a turn-down. Think of it more as a traffic solution.

> *(He stares at her.)*

You know, the bumping into each other.

ROBERTO. *(Smiles as he puts his arm around her.)* You are definitely one of a kind.

ANNIE. Yes, but what kind?

ROBERTO. The kind that makes me want to live as long as you do.

ANNIE. *(Snuggling up to him.)* That's nice.

> *(Lights begin to fade as chimes are heard.)*

ANNOUNCEMENT. *(Voice-over.)* Attention all residents! There will be a fire drill this afternoon at two p.m. If you think you might be napping, may we suggest you leave a wake-up call.

Scene Three

(Several weeks later – late afternoon.)

(The garden is a little greener. **PAUL** *is seated alone, reading his newspaper. Birds are chirping even louder than in spring.)*

PAUL. *(Looks up from his paper.)* Keep away, you miserable flying objects.

> *(***ROBERTO** *enters, wearing a different jacket, looking as sharp as ever.)*

ROBERTO. There you are. Just the man I want to see.

PAUL. Really?

ROBERTO. *(As he sits.)* You've no doubt observed how Annie and I have been warming up to each other the last few weeks.

PAUL. It's not exactly classified information.

ROBERTO. Well, I thought that since you've known her so long, you might be able to give me a few pointers on how best to approach her.

PAUL. I think you're way past the "approaching" phase.

ROBERTO. What I mean is, I think I may have made a wrong move.

PAUL. What kind of move?

ROBERTO. *(A beat.)* I asked her to marry me.

PAUL. That's not a move, that's a complete *relocate*. And what did she say?

ROBERTO. She turned me down.

PAUL. She's smarter than I thought.

> *(Quickly:)*

No offense. I simply mean, who gets married at this age?

ROBERTO. I would. What the hell, you only live once.

PAUL. Which is more than plenty.

ROBERTO. I realize, now that I met Annie, what I've been missing all these years. I mean, besides *everything*. I've been missing the excitement that comes with a new romance, the fluttering that goes on in your heart, the sizzling, the tingling...

PAUL. Sounds a lot like the shingles to me.

ROBERTO. I swear I can remember every single love I ever had, starting when I was seven. Angelina was her name.

> (**PAUL** *rolls his eyes.*)

She was so cute, so petite.

PAUL. Most women are at that age.

ROBERTO. I mean she was small for her age.

PAUL. Maybe she was only four.

ROBERTO. Are you accusing me of going out with a four-year-old?

PAUL. Just saying.

ROBERTO. What about you, Paul? What do you miss? Surely you miss *something.*

> (**PAUL** *puts his paper aside as his mood seems to change.*)

PAUL. I miss my Sylvie. And I miss our son, our only child. And now they're both gone.

> (*There's an awkward pause, then* **ROBERTO** *reaches for the kerchief in his jacket pocket and hands it to* **PAUL**, *who wipes his eyes and then blows his nose into it, then hands it back to* **ROBERTO**, *who's not quite sure what to do with it, finally deciding to put it back in the pocket.*)

ROBERTO. (*Takes a deep breath.*) Yes sir, I was looking forward to "wife number five."

PAUL. You were looking forward to a heart attack.

> (**ANNIE** *approaches, once again looking chic and full of energy.*)

ANNIE. Hello boys! And I use the term very lightly.

> (*As she nears bench,* **ROBERTO** *quickly gets up.* **PAUL** *tries to.*)

(To **PAUL**.*)* It's okay, it's the gesture that counts.

(She sits between them. **ROBERTO** *helps her sit.)*

ROBERTO. You look simply *ravishing* today.

ANNIE. *(Coyly.)* Why, thank you.

PAUL. *(Looks her over.)* So that's what ravishing looks like.

ANNIE. Those men are back.

ROBERTO. What men?

ANNIE. The ones who've been snooping around for months. There's a rumor going around that this place may be up for sale.

PAUL. It's more than a rumor. They've been taking pictures and measuring.

ROBERTO. *(Quickly gets up.)* Why don't I go have a talk with these people?

PAUL. A lot of good that'll do.

ROBERTO. *(With a twinkle in his eyes.)* I'm a very persuasive guy.

ANNIE. *(Shyly.)* I'll vouch for that

ROBERTO. *(To* **ANNIE**.*)* I'll see you at lunch.

(A beat.)

You too, Paul.

(He exits.)

ANNIE. That's what's known as a *doer*.

PAUL. Speaking of doers, maybe you could do something for me.

ANNIE. Like what?

PAUL. I have a question. As you know, I'm not one to beat around the bush. I say what I want to say, when I want to say it, and how I want to say it, and to whom I want to say it…

ANNIE. Is there a short version to this question?

PAUL. That dance that the "doer" managed to organize…

ANNIE. What about it?

PAUL. Well I was thinking of maybe going.

ANNIE. That's the spirit. Now you're talking.

PAUL. There's just one problem.

    (*A beat.*)

I can't dance. I always felt bad that my Sylvie wanted to dance and I couldn't.

ANNIE. (*As she gets up.*) And you'd like me to teach you?

PAUL. Not here.

ANNIE. Why not?

PAUL. Me and you? Here?

ANNIE. Who's going to stop us? We're senior citizens. We could go naked right now if we wanted to.

PAUL. Let's not push it.

    (*As he rises:*)

I'd like to start with the waltz if you don't mind.

ANNIE. The waltz it is.

    (*She extends her hand to* **PAUL** *as they move to the side.* **PAUL**'*s shoes are making a flapping sound.*)

What's with your shoes? Are they new?

PAUL. Sort of.

ANNIE. Why are they making so much noise?

PAUL. They're a little loose.

    (*He demonstrates.*)

ANNIE. Jimmy's family is upstairs, going crazy looking for his things.

    (*Looks down at* **PAUL**'*s shoes.*)

Are those Jimmy's?

PAUL. He willed them to me.

ANNIE. *He willed them to you?*

PAUL. He told me a few days before he died that he wanted me to have some of his things, including his shoes, because we're the same size...more or less.

ANNIE. What do you mean, more or less? You wear a nine, he wore a thirteen.

PAUL. A podiatrist once told me that your toes should be able to play the piano inside your shoes.

ANNIE. Why would anybody want to wear somebody else's shoes? Especially a dead person's shoes.

PAUL. Because they're comfortable.

ANNIE. They're *four* sizes too *big*!

PAUL. That's why they're comfortable.

ANNIE. *(Looks at his arm.)* And where'd you get that watch?

PAUL. What watch?

ANNIE. The one on your arm. You never wore a watch before.

PAUL. That's because I never believed in time.

ANNIE. And now you do?

PAUL. Well now I have a watch.

ANNIE. What else did he "will" you?

PAUL. Nothing else.

> *(A beat.)*

Just some cash.

ANNIE. You took money too?

PAUL. A few dollars that were crumpled up on the floor.

ANNIE. You are really *something*.

PAUL. The maids would have taken it anyway.

ANNIE. Let's get back to the waltz.

> *(Putting his right hand around her and holding his other hand with her right.)*

I'm going to propel the movement although you will ostensibly be leading. Understand?

PAUL. No.

ANNIE. Just follow me. One, two, three…

PAUL. Four.

ANNIE. There is no "four" with the waltz. It's just three. Here we go.

> *(She starts leading him as she moves backward.)*

ANNIE. One, two, three... One, two, three... One, two, three...

> *(**PAUL** joins her in counting:)*

PAUL & ANNIE. One, two, three... One, two, three...

> *(They're moving around awkwardly with **PAUL**'s shoe's flapping away.)*

ANNIE. You're doing very nicely. One, two, three... Don't look at your feet...

> *(**PAUL** looks at his feet.)*

Look at me. One, two, three... One, two, three...

> *(**ROBERTO** returns, looks at them for a few moments until they notice him and stop dancing.)*

ROBERTO. Seaside Heights has been sold!

> *(Blackout.)*

> *(Sound of the chimes.)*

ANNOUNCEMENT. *(Voice-over.)* Attention all residents! Dr. Arnold will be conducting a free hearing test in the main salon this afternoon. I said...

> *(Much louder:)*

DR. ARNOLD WILL BE CONDUCTING A FREE HEARING TEST IN THE MAIN SALON THIS AFTERNOON!

Scene Four

(Several weeks later – morning.)

*(**PAUL** is seated, reading his paper as usual. He's now wearing regular shoes. **ANNIE** enters, as spry as ever. She approaches the bench. He hears her coming, turns around.)*

ANNIE. How come you're up so early?

PAUL. Old man Fletcher came into my room by mistake and lay down next to me.

(A beat.)

I think it was a mistake.

*(**ANNIE** laughs and sits.)*

I haven't seen you work on your memoirs recently

ANNIE. I'm taking a break. Letting my thoughts rest for awhile. Allowing my brain to relax.

PAUL. Yeah, well, be careful it doesn't turn to Jell-O.

ANNIE. Do you forget who you're talking to? My mind is as sharp as ever. And don't kid yourself, the mind is *everything*. Eating, drinking, making love...it's all up here.

(Indicates her head.)

Used to be somewhere else but...

PAUL. *(Quickly.)* I get it.

(A beat.)

I suppose you saw the list they posted?

ANNIE. What list?

PAUL. The list of potential places for us to move to.

ANNIE. Who says we're moving?

PAUL. Annie, open your eyes. Stop pretending you can't see what's going on around you.

ANNIE. Roberto says he may have a solution.

PAUL. *(Dismissing.)* Oh, please.

ANNIE. What have you got against him? So far, he's arranged for us to have a dance, we went to Atlantic City, he organized that whole Fourth of July picnic...

> *(Reaches for her iPhone.)*

Did I ever show you the pictures?

PAUL. The dance, the trip or the picnic?

ANNIE. All of it. Remember this?

> *(They both look at phone.)*

That's when I hit the nickle jackpot.

PAUL. Where am I?

ANNIE. Probably in the john, where you spend most of your leisure time.

PAUL. Who's the old lady?

ANNIE. That's old man Fletcher.

PAUL. *(Surprised.)* I never saw him wear a dress before.

ANNIE. It was his "coming out" dress. There's Roberto. He looks so debonair, so sophisticated, so "man of the world."

PAUL. He's dressed exactly like the croupier.

> *(A beat.)*

Is it true he asked you to marry him?

ANNIE. Who told you that?

PAUL. The groom.

ANNIE. I wasn't going to tell you.

PAUL. Why not? You told me about all the others.

> *(A beat.)*

Why'd you turn him down?

ANNIE. *(Thinks for a moment.)* I'm not really sure why.

> *(Back to her phone.)*

Want to see yourself on the dance floor?

> *(**PAUL** leans in closer.)*

That's you, dancing with Mrs. Gerrin.

PAUL. Why is she making that face?

ANNIE. Maybe because you're doing the waltz while they're playing a rap song.

PAUL. Rap and song don't belong in the same sentence.

ANNIE. I disagree with you. I've heard some rap that was very profound and very meaningful.

PAUL. Then how come every second word rhymes with truck?

ANNIE. Okay, no more pictures.

(She puts her phone away. **PAUL** *takes out a piece of paper.)*

PAUL. Do you want to see some of the places they're suggesting? These are all in New Jersey. There's one near Point Pleasant. It's called Point Pleasant Acres. I guarantee it's not pleasant and it's way less than an acre.

ANNIE. What about the point?

PAUL. There is no point. There's no point to any of this.

ANNIE. Then why are you getting all agitated?

PAUL. I'm not agitated, I'm stating the facts. Here's another one. This one is called Valley View Gardens.

ANNIE. Let me guess. There's no valley.

PAUL. No view.

ANNIE. And a lousy garden.

PAUL. Now you're catching on. The names they give these places. "Summerhill Terrace," "Wintergarden Meadow," "Oaklawn Vista."

ANNIE. You know the rule. The fancier the name, the fancier the price.

PAUL. Now, if they had something called "Cell Block Eleven."

ANNIE. There must be a way to time it just right. You have so much money and then the day you run out of it, you drop dead.

PAUL. It's a crazy system. They do everything to keep you alive but very little to keep you living.

ANNIE. You know, if I had to move again, I'd want it to be closer to Manhattan. Somewhere like Nyack or Poughkeepsie.

PAUL. What's the difference? You never go to New York.

ANNIE. But I'd still like to be near. It's where I spent all of my married life. With Adam, we lived on Central Park West. With Bernie, we lived on Central Park South and with Charles, we lived on Park Avenue. Not bad for a girl from Columbus, huh?

PAUL. You know what I never understood about you, Annie? You married three super rich guys and yet you still wound up here.

ANNIE. I guess I had to prove to myself that I didn't marry for money.

PAUL. *(Shakes his head.)* Well, you proved it to me.

> *(Goes back to his paper).*

ANNIE. *(Takes a deep breath.)* Do you realize this is the first day of the rest of our lives?

PAUL. *(Putting down his paper.)* Are you trying to depress me?

ANNIE. Did you see that baby who came to visit someone yesterday? The cutest thing I've ever seen. He was just starting to walk.

PAUL. And we're just stopping.

ANNIE. It's the circle of life, Paul. We leave, the young replace us. Although I have a feeling we come back.

PAUL. Is that so?

ANNIE. Maybe as something else.

PAUL. Anything in particular?

ANNIE. I don't know, maybe some nice friendly animal like a lamb or a deer.

PAUL. No rodents?

ANNIE. *(Repulsed.)* No, of course not.

PAUL. I hate to be the one to break this to you, Annie, but when it ends it ends.

ANNIE. You're so negative.

PAUL. I'm not negative, I'm just observant. I've watched every single year that I've been on earth, and so far, no one has ever come back from *anywhere*. That's why it's called "the end." If it wasn't, they'd call it "be right back." But they don't, they call it "the end."

ANNIE. You know what? I think you're afraid of the hereafter.

PAUL. What if I told you that there's only a "here" and no "after."

ANNIE. If there's no hereafter, then there's probably no one in charge up there, correct?

PAUL. I didn't say that.

ANNIE. And if the Great Coordinator doesn't exist, then just how do you explain these trees and these bushes and these flowers?

PAUL. Freaks of nature.

ANNIE. And Niagara Falls?

PAUL. A wetter freak of nature.

ANNIE. I think you're a freak of nature.

PAUL. You're right. Me, you, we're all freaks of nature.

ANNIE. *(Calls off.)* Roberto!

PAUL. Let me explain this, if I may. In the beginning, the universe exploded. Bada bing, bada bang! Particles flew all over the place. Some of it got together and formed this slime. All of a sudden, the slime started to swim, then it started to crawl. It developed arms and legs, then ears and a nose, and, eventually, that slime turned into us!

ANNIE. *(Calls off.)* Roberto!

　　　(Starts getting up.)

I don't have to listen to this. It's a free country.

PAUL. Yes, free but expensive.

　　　*(**ROBERTO**, as dapper as ever, comes running in.)*

ROBERTO. Were you calling me?

ANNIE. Thank God, you're here. Paul is having one of his meltdowns.

PAUL. I'm not down and I'm not melting.

ROBERTO. Well, this may cheer everybody up. I made some phone calls and I'm happy to report that a few people still remember who I was. I think I may have a way to save Seaside Heights Manor.

ANNIE. *(Excited.)* You do?

ROBERTO. It's a bit of a long shot but I think it's worth it.

PAUL. Long shots are called long shots for a reason.

ANNIE. Why don't we just listen to him?

ROBERTO. Thank you. This documentary company is very interested in talking to all of you about how unfair it is to give such short notice. They'll want to know about your background, your families, how you wound up here. They're also interested in possibly exposing what you people in this country call…"shenanigans" that may have gone on with the sale of this property. They're here now. I have to get back to them.

> *(He rushes out.)*

PAUL. You mean they're going to do a documentary about us? They're going to pry into our personal lives? That's an invasion of privacy. I'll sue.

ANNIE. Come on, Paul, it's a chance for you to voice your opinion. You can complain about the staff, the service, the food. It'll be as if you'd died and went to "complaint heaven."

PAUL. Who's going to listen to a bunch of old "fuddy-duddies"?

ANNIE. They might, if you weren't such an old fuddy-duddy.

PAUL. Do we get paid for this?

ANNIE. I imagine if you're interviewed, you get a token fee.

PAUL. What if we're just in the background?

ANNIE. I don't think they pay you for that.

PAUL. I'll sue.

> *(Gets up.)*

I'll bet you most of the documentary will revolve around him.

ANNIE. So what? As long as we benefit from it, what do we care?

PAUL. I'd like to know why he's doing all this for us?

ANNIE. All stars like to have a cause.

PAUL. Well I don't need his charity.

(He exits as **ROBERTO** *rushes back in.)*

ROBERTO. Where's Paul going?

ANNIE. To his room, I guess.

ROBERTO. Is something the matter?

ANNIE. I think this whole thing is bringing back memories of his wife and son.

ROBERTO. He told me about that.

ANNIE. Did he tell you about the car accident?

ROBERTO. No.

ANNIE. And that he was driving at the time?

ROBERTO. No, he didn't.

(Shakes his head.)

Poor guy.

(Helps **ANNIE** *up.)*

Come! I think they're ready for you.

ANNIE. *(As she gets up.)* Gee, I don't know how to talk to cameras.

ROBERTO. It's nothing. All you have to do is speak from the heart, relax and sit up straight.

ANNIE. I might be able to do one of those.

(The two of them start to exit.)

I must say, this is all very exciting. And it's all being coordinated by the man upstairs.

ROBERTO. You mean the producer?

ANNIE. Yes, you can call Him that.

(Lights quickly fade as chimes are heard.)

ANNOUNCEMENT. *(Voice-over.)* Attention all residents! A pill box containing dozens of pills had been found in the lobby. These are the initials on the box. S-M-T-W-T-F...never mind.

Scene Five

(A month later – morning.)

*(***PAUL*** *is at one end of the bench, trying to lift it. His newspaper is folded and laid out on the bench. A long walking stick is leaning against the bench.* ***ANNIE*** *enters. She's wearing a raincoat and holding two closed umbrellas.)*

ANNIE. What are you doing?

PAUL. I'm trying to move the bench to get out of the sun.

ANNIE. What sun? It's going to rain.

PAUL. Who told you that?

ANNIE. My phone. It tells me everything.

PAUL. Well, your phone is wrong. My knee is the one who tells me when it's going to rain and so far, my knee is silent.

ANNIE. Which knee, the old one or the replacement?

PAUL. The old one. The replacement doesn't talk.

ANNIE. *(Placing the two umbrellas on the bench.)* Anyway, I brought these just in case.

    (Notices stick.)

Is this your cane?

PAUL. It's called a walking stick.

ANNIE. I suppose when you get a wheelchair you'll call it a car. How do you like it?

PAUL. It's too long. It's only good when I'm going downhill.

    (Indicates bench.)

Are you going to help me with this or not?

ANNIE. You're serious about this?

PAUL. I'm serious about everything

ANNIE. Don't I know it.

PAUL. Just grab your end. I'll count to three. Here we go.

ANNIE. Who made you the leader?

PAUL. Somebody has to be in charge. That's how things get done. You notice there aren't five presidents of the United States, there's only one.

ANNIE. Five presidents is not such a bad idea. One to do the job, and the other four to apologize for him.

PAUL. Just lift your end.

> (**ANNIE** *tries to lift as* **PAUL** *struggles to lift his end. Nothing happens.*)
>
> (*Excited:*)

We did it! We moved it!

ANNIE. We did?

PAUL. Yes, at least a quarter inch.

ANNIE. Is that the plan, a quarter inch a day? By next year we will have made a complete circle.

PAUL. By next year, God knows where we'll be.

ANNIE. Don't worry so much. Roberto is on the case. As soon as that documentary hits the air everything could change.

PAUL. Where is Roberto today?

ANNIE. Didn't you hear? The second floor is quarantined.

PAUL. What is it, the plague?

ANNIE. It's the flu.

PAUL. I thought we all got shots for that.

ANNIE. Maybe he wasn't here yet when we got our shots. Do you remember when we got our shots?

PAUL. I don't even remember *getting* a shot.

ANNIE. Well, you did. You held on to me so tightly I was bruised for a week.

> (*Shows her upper arm.*)

PAUL. (*Looks closely.*) I don't see anything.

ANNIE. That's 'cause it's been three months.

PAUL. I don't like needles, I don't like nurses and I especially don't like doctors

ANNIE. You don't have to like them, you just have to listen to them.

PAUL. *You* listen to them. And you can tell me later what they said.

ANNIE. *(Puts her hand out.)* Oh, oh, it's starting to drizzle.

> *(Hands him one of the umbrellas.)*

Here, take this.

> *(They both open their umbrellas that are banging into each other.)*

PAUL. This isn't working. You'll have to lower yours so mine can be on top.

ANNIE. Oh, I forgot, you're the leader.

> *(They proceed to do just that.)*

I love the rain.

PAUL. You love everything.

ANNIE. It feels like we're at an old college football game.

PAUL. Funny, to me it feels like we're at an old people's home.

ANNIE. I'd rather pretend I'm twenty. Wouldn't you like to be twenty again?

PAUL. No thanks. The last time I was twenty you left me for that millionaire jerk.

ANNIE. Come on, Paul, you told me a long time ago that I probably did you the biggest favor ever.

PAUL. True, but I still wouldn't want to be twenty again.

ANNIE. Well, I would. I liked being twenty. I've been twenty at least three times.

> *(**PAUL** looks at her.)*

I was twenty when I was twenty. When I was fifteen I pretended to be twenty and when I was thirty-five I still pretended to be twenty. The truth is I've been happy at all ages. I'm even happy right now.

PAUL. *(Looks up at his umbrella.)* I'm getting wet here.

ANNIE. How can that be? You're covered by two umbrellas.

PAUL. This thing has a hole in it.

> *(Examines handle.)*

This isn't my umbrella. I don't have a handle like this.

ANNIE. Then what was it doing in your room?

PAUL. *(Indignant.)* What were you doing in my room?

ANNIE. How else was I supposed to get your umbrella?

PAUL. I don't like people going into my room.

ANNIE. You have such private things in your room?

PAUL. It's *my* room.

ANNIE. You're in room thirty-eight, right?

PAUL. I'm in thirty-six.

ANNIE. Then who's in thirty-eight?

PAUL. That's old man Fletcher.

> *(Hands over his umbrella.)* Here, take it back.

ANNIE. But you'll get wet.

PAUL. Wet is better than being attacked by old man Fletcher.

ANNIE. *(Holds hand out.)* I think it stopped.

> *(She closes both umbrellas and takes out her
> yellow pad from her bag. He goes back to his
> newspaper. She starts writing.)*

PAUL. Still working on your memoirs?

ANNIE. You bet. I'm almost caught up to the present. Now
I'm waiting to see how that documentary pans out.

PAUL. When is that supposed to be on?

ANNIE. I think Roberto said a week from Tuesday.

PAUL. I'm sure the millionaires who bought this place are
going to watch the documentary and say: "Look at
those poor people. Let's not make more millions, let's
let those nice old people stay where they are."

ANNIE. You never know.

PAUL. Yes, of course you know. If you stopped living in a
dream world, you'd know.

ANNIE. You call it a dream world, I call it reality. I still say
we're luckier than most people. We have a roof over our
heads, at least till now. We're relatively healthy. We live
in a world filled with brilliant musicians and artists,

and doctors and regular everyday folks who do all sorts of kind and wonderful things for one another.

(**PAUL** *gets up, grabs his newspaper, and picks up his walking stick.*)

Where are you going?

PAUL. *(As he leaves.)* I'm gonna go write a letter to Santa Claus and ask him not to bother bringing anything next Christmas.

(He exits.)

ANNIE. *(Looks up at the heavens.)* Forgive him, for he knows not what he's doing.

(Lights quickly fade. Sound of the chimes.)

ANNOUNCEMENT. *(Voice-over.)* Attention everyone! The Suggestion Box is missing again. Will the person who took it kindly return it. And that's more than a suggestion.

Scene Six

(Early September – afternoon.)

(The bench is empty. Some of the leaves have turned to red and yellow. We hear the sound of a siren becoming more distant till it disappears. ANNIE and PAUL approach the bench together. PAUL is now using one of those four-pronged canes.)

ANNIE. Do you think he'll be alright?

PAUL. Who knows! He's been under a lot of pressure lately.

ANNIE. Poor guy. Just when he was starting to feel comfortable wearing a dress.

> *(They sit. PAUL places his cane on the ground next to him.)*

PAUL. *(Indicates cane.)* See that? My cane can stand upright but I can't.

ANNIE. *(Looks down at cane.)* That's because you only have two legs.

> *(PAUL opens his newspaper. ANNIE reaches into her bag and takes out that red knitting that is now much wider and stretches even longer than before.)*

PAUL. You still working on that?

ANNIE. I'm almost finished.

PAUL. Looks like you went from a sweater to a blanket.

ANNIE. You're just jealous.

PAUL. Yeah, sure. So, how was the documentary?

ANNIE. You mean you didn't see it?

PAUL. I don't spend my lifetime glued to the TV set. I very seldom watch. And when I do it's mostly the news.

ANNIE. Don't make me laugh. I've never walked by your room when you weren't on your knees with your face up against the screen. If I didn't know better I'd think you were praying.

PAUL. I'm adjusting the color.

ANNIE. Black and white are not colors.

PAUL. So what was the thrust of the piece?

ANNIE. Well, basically, they said that senior citizens deserve to live too.

PAUL. Gee, who came up with that radical notion?

ANNIE. The best part was watching Anderson Cooper sample the lentil soup.

PAUL. I suppose Roberto was all over the screen.

ANNIE. Of course. It was his project and he looked *good.* Just like a movie star.

> (**ROBERTO** *enters, holding a small birthday cake with a few candles on it and a paper bag.*)

ROBERTO.
HAPPY BIRTHDAY TO YOU
HAPPY BIRTHDAY TO YOU
HAPPY BIRTHDAY DEAR ANNIE
HAPPY BIRTHDAY TO YOU

> (*He places the cake on the bench and gives* **ANNIE** *a kiss on the cheek.*)

Happy Birthday, Annie.

> (*During the following,* **ROBERTO** *proceeds to take out plastic forks, paper plates, and paper napkins from the bag and hand them out.*)

PAUL. Yeah, Happy Birthday.

ANNIE. How sweet! But it's not my birthday till June.

ROBERTO. What's the difference? A cake by any other name is still a cake.

PAUL. (*A puzzled look on his face.*) Okay.

> (*A beat, then looking at candles:*)

Aren't those supposed to be lit?

ROBERTO. They were but the wind blew them out.

(To **ANNIE**.*)* You'll just have to pretend when you make your wish.

ANNIE. What do you wish for at my age?

PAUL. Another birthday.

ROBERTO. Go ahead, blow them out.

> *(***ANNIE*** closes her eyes and "blows" out the nonexistent flames.)*

Hooray!

PAUL. I hate rituals. That's probably why I never belonged to any formal religion.

ANNIE. Look how he manages to connect a simple act of blowing out candles to religion.

ROBERTO. *(Taking knife from his jacket pocket.)* The first piece goes to the birthday girl.

> *(He proceeds to cut a slice and puts it on a paper plate.)*

PAUL. Another ritual.

> *(***ROBERTO*** cuts ***PAUL*** a piece, as well as one for himself.)*

ANNIE. *(Takes a bite.)* This is the best cake I've had in years. It's also the only cake I've had in years, so you can't go by me.

ROBERTO. I'll never forget the cake we got Mickey Rooney one year. It was bigger than him. He went to cut it and a chorus girl jumped out. I think he married her.

> *(A beat.)*

I'd like to propose a toast.

PAUL. With what?

ROBERTO. With our imagination. Come on, hold up your glasses.

> *(He and ***ANNIE*** raise their cupped empty hands and look at ***PAUL***, who reluctantly does the same.)*

To Annie! May you continue to age with grace and beauty.

ANNIE. Thank you.

>   *(She and **ROBERTO** simulate taking a sip.*
>   ***PAUL** does likewise, then makes a face.)*

PAUL. *(Quietly.)* Lousy year.

>   *(Then, quickly:)*

Just kidding.

>   *(Takes another "sip.")*

ROBERTO. You know, when I made my first movie, way back when, they gave me my own chair with my name on the back. That chair meant a lot to me. But I think this bench means even more to me now. I'm so glad you included me in your group.

PAUL. What group? There are only three of us.

ANNIE. We're more than happy that you joined our group.

PAUL. I hate groups. I hate all groups. When I first arrived here, a bunch of the guys who had prostate problems had a group. You needed a PSA of five or better to join.

ANNIE. That was a joke by that comedian a few weeks ago.

PAUL. Yeah, well this isn't. When I was a kid I refused to join the Boy Scouts. The moment you put a few people together they start believing they have the answers and everybody else is wrong. I hate groups.

ANNIE. Are you finished?

PAUL. Yes, for now.

ROBERTO. Well, let's hope the reaction to our documentary does the trick and we all live happily ever after at Seaside Heights Manor.

PAUL. No offense, Roberto, but you're not a miracle worker.

ANNIE. *(Coyly.)* I don't know about that.

>   *(Then, to **ROBERTO**:)*

I'm convinced you were sent here for a purpose. Everything God puts on earth has a purpose.

PAUL. Oh, really?

ANNIE. Yes, everything, including all the people, all the vegetation and certain animals.

ROBERTO. Certain animals? Do you have a list?

ANNIE. Well, what I mean is that nice animals like cats and dogs, raccoons and birds are here because God wanted them here. But certain other animals, like small gray things that scare the heck out of you, and are ugly beyond belief...I think those evolved on their own.

ROBERTO. Paul, you want to jump in here?

PAUL. I think I ate a candle.

ANNIE. How do you eat a candle? Couldn't you feel something stringy?

PAUL. I thought it was part of the cake.

ROBERTO. But you said you liked the cake.

PAUL. I do. It's a terrific cake, except for the taste of candles.

ANNIE. *(Shakes her head.)* The man eats candles.

PAUL. *(Showing his napkin with part of it missing.)* I think I ate part of my napkin too.

ANNIE. You ate cake, a candle and a napkin, you'll probably want to skip dinner.

ROBERTO. As long as you didn't swallow your fork. You do still have your fork, don't you?

PAUL. *(Checks his throat for a moment, then looks down at bench.)* Here it is.

ROBERTO. Does anybody want more?

ANNIE. No thanks. I still have my napkin and my candle to eat.

> (**PAUL** *coughs and clears his throat.*)

ROBERTO. Is the candle stuck?

PAUL. I think it's the paper. Can paper kill you?

ANNIE. Only if you read it every day.

> (**PAUL**'s *cough is now more pronounced.*)

(Concerned.) Should we get a doctor?

PAUL. No doctor. I have two rules. No tapioca pudding and no doctors. I'm okay now.

(The coughing has subsided.)

ROBERTO. I'll take your fork. For safety reasons.

(Reaches for PAUL's fork.)

PAUL. I'd like to keep it...as a momento.

ANNIE. Paul, that's the sweetest thing ever.

ROBERTO. Shouldn't we be taking pictures?

ANNIE. *(Quickly getting up.)* I'll do it. I have my phone.

(Holds it up.)

PAUL. No, no, you sit. I'll take one of the two of you.

(Takes phone from her, gets up and holds it in front of his eyes.)

ANNIE. Not like that. You're going to take a picture of yourself.

(She turns it around for PAUL, then to ROBERTO:)

How do I look?

ROBERTO. Like a movie queen.

PAUL. How about a little cheesecake?

ROBERTO. No more cake, thank you.

ANNIE. I think he means he wants to see more of my legs.

ROBERTO. Good idea.

(Reaches down for her skirt and pulls it up a little.)

ANNIE. *(With mock indignation.)* Roberto!

(She gets up.)

I have an idea.

(Gets phone from PAUL.)

I think there's a timer on this. Maybe we can get a picture of the three of us.

(She looks around and goes to nearby trash can, sets the timer, and props up the phone

on the trash can. Then she runs back to the bench and sits between them. The three of them smile. When they speak they hardly move their lips.)

PAUL. How long does it take?

ANNIE. I don't know. I've never used it before.

ROBERTO. My jaw is locking.

PAUL. My ass is falling asleep.

ANNIE. Let's forget it.

(She gets up and retrieves her iPhone.)

We'll get someone inside to take it later. Now let's clean up this mess.

ROBERTO. We'll do it. You sit down and relax.

PAUL. We'll?

ROBERTO. You don't have to. I got it.

(He proceeds to quickly dump everything into the bag.)

ANNIE. I'll bet Mickey Rooney's cake wasn't this good. This may be the best birthday I ever had.

PAUL. And it's not even your birthday.

(Sound of the chimes.)

ANNOUNCEMENT. *(Voice-over.)* Attention everyone! We have a very special film presentation this evening at seven, starring none other than our own Roberto Delarosa...

ROBERTO. How embarrassing.

ANNOUNCEMENT. *(Voice-over.)* ...In a fully restored version of *Beach Bongo Blast.* See you there.

ROBERTO. *(To* **ANNIE**.*)* Please don't go.

ANNIE. Why not? It'll be fun.

PAUL. We get to see you in swim trunks.

ROBERTO. I was a kid. I was all skin and bones.

ANNIE. Maybe they'll have a Q and A after.

PAUL. I'll bet I can come up with a couple of questions.

ROBERTO. *(Hurries off.)* I'm going to go make sure they don't do that.

> *(He exits.)*

ANNIE. I just love European men. That's probably why I always had trouble looking at American men.

PAUL. What are you talking about? You married three of them.

ANNIE. I married them but I didn't look at them.

PAUL. *(Smiles, points to her.)* Last week's comic?

ANNIE. *(Smiles.)* No, two weeks ago. What time is it?

PAUL. *(Looks at his watch.)* I have no idea, It stopped working last month.

ANNIE. Then why do you wear it?

PAUL. It has the correct time twice a day.

ANNIE. *(Shakes her head.)* Shall we?

> *(She gets up.)*

PAUL. *(Also gets up and reaches for his cane.)* Do I have a choice?

> *(They start walking away.)*
>
> *(Lights start to fade.)*
>
> *(Sound of the chimes.)*

ANNOUNCEMENT. *(Voice-over.)* Attention everyone! A shoe, size thirteen, has been found in the jacuzzi. We can't tell if it's the right foot or the left.

PAUL. It's the left.

ANNIE. What did you do with the other one?

PAUL. I'm using it as a planter.

ANNOUNCEMENT. *(Voice-over.)* The shoe is drying in the sauna.

Scene Seven

(Late September – afternoon.)

(The trees are practically bare. It's cloudy. **ANNIE** *walks out first. She's wearing a shawl.)*

ANNIE. *(Calling back.)* Come on, it's not that cold.

> *(***PAUL,*** *now using a walker, walks out. He's wearing a bright-red sweater that's much too big for him. The sleeves actually cover his hands. They both approach the bench.)*

That color looks good on you.

> *(She sits. He places walker next to him and sits.)*

PAUL. *(As he looks at his sleeves.)* I can see why Roberto turned it down.

ANNIE. He didn't turn it down. He never got a chance to see it.

PAUL. Why would somebody leave like that? No forwarding address. Nothing.

ANNIE. Well, he did leave me a note.

PAUL. He did? Why didn't you tell me?

ANNIE. *(As she takes it out.)* It's kind of personal.

PAUL. *(Reaching for it.)* Let me see that.

ANNIE. I'll read it, if you don't mind. "My dearest, sweetest Annie. Sorry to have left in such a haste."

PAUL. He would use the word haste instead of rush.

ANNIE. "I thought it better to leave this way. You'll never know the impact you had on me."

PAUL. What am I, chopped liver?

ANNIE. "I promise to never forget you as I continue my journey. And I hope your journey is filled with wonder, discovery and joy." Signed, "Dino Delarosa, my real name."

PAUL. I knew it. I knew it.

ANNIE. I like Roberto better. "P.S. Say goodbye to Paul."

PAUL. *(Grabs the note.)* Let me see that.

> *(Reads.)*

I thought you were kidding about that part.

> *(Gives it back to her.)*

Are you sure he didn't leave a forwarding address at the desk?

ANNIE. No, not a word.

PAUL. Where do you think he went?

ANNIE. Maybe he went back to Italy to track down his son and daughter.

PAUL. Maybe he went back to Hollywood.

ANNIE. I don't think so.

PAUL. Do you think he knew all along he was planning to leave like that?

ANNIE. That could explain my birthday party. I guess we should be grateful for the time he did spend with us. He was like our guardian angel.

PAUL. Did I ever tell you about the time I made him laugh?

ANNIE. *(Surprised.)* You made him laugh?

PAUL. I told him I had just come back from the doctor's and the doctor said I was in perfect health and that I could do anything I want...but it better be this week.

ANNIE. *(Laughs.)* I don't remember any comedian doing that joke.

PAUL. I made it up myself.

ANNIE. Congratulations! See? I'll bet Roberto brought that out in you.

PAUL. Well, at least our picketing days are over and I've signed my last petition. And, best of all, I don't have to write any more damn letters to AARP.

ANNIE. He sure stirred things up around here.

PAUL. In the meantime we're still being evacuated.

ANNIE. *Relocated*, not evacuated. There's a big difference. And thanks to Roberto we're winding up at the same place.

PAUL. Pineview Mansion! I guarantee there isn't a pine in sight.

ANNIE. Yes, I know, and the mansion is probably half the size of this place.

    (Looks around.)

I wish I could've spent one more Christmas here.

PAUL. Why?

ANNIE. I don't know. This place looked pretty with snow around it.

PAUL. There'll be snow at the new place. It's only eight miles from here.

ANNIE. Are you finished packing?

PAUL. Almost. How are we getting there?

ANNIE. I think we should arrive there in style. I ordered a limo.

PAUL. Whoa!

ANNIE. People respect you more if they think you have money.

    (They both get up. **PAUL** *looks at the bench and taps it.)*

PAUL. I never thought I'd say this but I'm gonna miss you. Through thick and thin, through sunshine and rain, through good days and bad days...

ANNIE. You can cut the clichés, I made arrangements to have it shipped to our new place.

PAUL. You did?

ANNIE. That way we'll have something to remember Roberto by.

PAUL. Yeah, his rear end.

ANNIE. Better than nothing.

    (They start to walk away.)

PAUL. I'm thinking of getting an electric wheelchair at the new place.

ANNIE. Let me know in advance so I'll keep off the pathways.

(A beat.)

I've decided when I die, I'm leaving everything to you.

PAUL. *(A beat.)* And I'll leave everything to you.

ANNIE. You got the better deal.

(Lights are fading.)

Want a banana?

PAUL. Do you have two of them?

ANNIE. Why, do you want two of them? I offered you a banana, do you want it or not?

(Lights fade.)

End of Play

COSTUME PLOT

Scene One
PAUL: Pajamas, robe, socks, slippers
ANNIE: Smart outfit, chic
ROBERTO: Pants and jacket, kerchief in jacket pocket

Scene Two
ANNIE: A slight variation of what she wore earlier
PAUL: Now wearing regular pants with a sweater but still in slippers
ROBERTO: Still dapper. A different jacket and pants

Scene Three
PAUL: Slight variation. Now wearing loose-fitting loafers and a watch
ROBERTO: Yet another impeccable jacket
ANNIE: New outfit, still chic

Scene Four
PAUL: Now wearing regular shoes
ANNIE: Tasteful jacket
ROBERTO: Another stylish jacket

Scene Five
PAUL: Dressed as usual
ANNIE: Wearing a raincoat and carrying two black umbrellas

Scene Six
ANNIE: Wearing something a little heavier but tasteful
PAUL: Looking the same but now using a four-pronged cane
ROBERTO: Smart-looking attire

Scene Seven

ANNIE: Now wearing a shawl covering her shoulders

PAUL: Has on a bright-red sweater, extra long sleeves, much too big on him

PROPERTY PLOT

Scene One

Park bench. Dark green wooden planks. Heavy concrete arms and legs.

Trash can right

Various bushes, shrubs and trees

Street light downright

Walkway that curves in front of bench and goes off in both directions

Set:

Newspaper

Set offstage left:

Apple

iPhone

Scene Two

Set offstage right:

Writing pad

Ballpoint pen

Knitting in bag – long, bright-red narrow piece of wool

Large scrapbook album

Scene Three

Add some flowers to bushes. Bushes are greener and birds are chirping.

Set:

Newspaper

Set offstage right:

Loose-fitting loafers

Wristwatch

Scene Four

More colorful flowers in the bushes

Set:
Newspaper
Set offstage right:
iPhone
Piece of paper

Scene Five
Set:
Newspaper
Walking stick
Set offstage right:
Two black umbrellas – closed
Handbag with writing pad and ballpoint pen

Scene Six
Fewer flowers. Some trees have gone from green to yellow.
Set offstage right:
A four-pronged cane
Newspaper
Handbag with knitting now considerably longer
A paper bag containing paper plates and napkins with
 plastic forks
A small knife

Scene Seven
Trees are almost bare – flowers all gone
Strike:
Cake, bag with plates and forks
Set offstage right:
A walker
Piece of paper (a note)
Banana
The set can be close to the set for *A Bench in the Sun* but
without the tree stump.

www.ingramcontent.com/pod-product-compliance
Lightning Source LLC
Chambersburg PA
CBHW070400120726
47909CB00008B/2925